■ ■ ■ ■ ■ ■ ■ ■ ■ ■

Junie B., First Grader
Boss of Lunch

BARBARA PARK

Junie B., First Grader
Boss of Lunch

illustrated by Denise Brunkus

SCHOLASTIC INC.

New York Toronto London Auckland Sydney
Mexico City New Delhi Hong Kong Buenos Aires

No part of this publication may be reproduced in whole or in part,
or stored in a retrieval system, or transmitted in any form or by any means,
electronic, mechanical, photocopying, recording, or otherwise,
without written permission of the publisher.
For information regarding permission, write to Random House
Children's Books, a division of Random House, Inc.,
1540 Broadway, 20th floor, New York, NY 10036.

ISBN 0-439-49864-3

Text copyright © 2002 by Barbara Park.
Illustrations copyright © 2002 by Denise Brunkus.
All rights reserved.
Published by Scholastic Inc., 557 Broadway, New York, NY 10012,
by arrangement with Random House Children's Books,
a division of Random House, Inc. SCHOLASTIC and associated logos
are trademarks and/or registered trademarks of Scholastic Inc.

12 11 10 9   10 11 12 13 14 15/0

Printed in the U.S.A.   40

First Scholastic printing, January 2003

For cafeteria workers far and wide.
We love you guys!

Contents

■ ■ ■ ■ ■ ■ ■ ■ ■ ■

Junie B., First Grader
Boss of Lunch

1

■ ■ ■ ■ ■ ■ ■ ■ ■ ■

Not Normal

Thursday

Dear first-grade journal,

Hurray! Hurray! It came! It finally came!

Yesterday the delivery man brought it right to my house! And today I carried it to school for the very first time!

Right now it is sitting under my desk. I keep ~~sneeking~~ sneaking down there to see it closer. But my teacher just said to please stop doing that.

Only guess what? He is not even watching me right now. So I think I will sneak down there one more time. And that will be it, possibly.

I wish myself good luck.

From,

Junie B., First Grader

I put down my pencil and looked all around.

Room One was still writing in their journals.

I smiled very sneaky.

Then I bent over in my chair real slow.

And I reached way down. And I lifted up the lid of my brand-new, shiny—

"LUNCH BOX!" hollered out May. "JUNIE JONES JUST OPENED HER LUNCH BOX AGAIN, MR. SCARY! AND YOU TOLD HER NOT TO DO THAT ANYMORE! REMEMBER?"

May is the tattletale girl who sits next to me.

I do not actually care for her.

My heart pounded very hard. I bent over even more. And I hid my head so my teacher couldn't see me.

Only I didn't do a good job of hiding, I guess. Because just then, I heard Mr. Scary's shoes walking toward me.

"Junie B.? Why is your lunch box open

again?" asked Mr. Scary. "Didn't I just speak to you about this a few minutes ago?"

I kept my head down and I looked at the floor. One of Mr. Scary's shoes started tapping at me.

Tappy shoes are not happy shoes, I think.

"Junie B.?" said Mr. Scary again. "Do you have a good reason for opening your lunch box again?"

I quick closed my eyes and tried to think of a good reason.

Mr. Scary's shoe tapped louder.

I opened my eyes and peeked at it.

And then, BINGO!

All of a sudden, a miracle happened!

One of my eyes saw my napkin in the corner of my lunch box . . . and a bright idea popped right into my head!

I quick grabbed the napkin. And I started shining Mr. Scary's shoes!

"Look, Mr. Scary! Look! Here is my

good reason!" I said. "See me? Huh? I am shining your shoes with my napkin. See?"

I shined and shined.

"This is the smartest reason I ever came up with," I said very proud.

I smiled up at him. "Would you like some spit on the napkin?" I asked real nice. "A little spit makes shoes look extra gleamy."

Mr. Scary quick pulled his shoe away.

"No, Junie B. No spit. *Please*. Just sit up," he said.

I sat up.

Mr. Scary stared and stared at me.

I wiggled in my seat very uncomfortable. 'Cause staring teachers make me squirmy, of course.

Finally, Mr. Scary talked again.

"I want you to stay *out* of your lunch box, Junie B.," he said. "We have a rule in

Room One. Lunch boxes are to be opened *only* in the cafeteria."

I did a sad sigh.

"Yes," I said. "I know the rule, Mr. Scary. But I waited a real long time to get this lunch box. And yesterday it finally came to my house. And so today is my first day of not carrying a plain brown sack to school. And so every time I look at that new lunch box, I feel happy inside."

I picked it up to show him.

"See how cute it is?" I said. "My mother ordered it from a nature store. It has pictures of baby birds on it. See all of them?"

I pointed. "This one is my favorite," I said. "It is called an owlet. *Owlet* is the name for a baby owl. My grampa Frank Miller told me that."

I pointed at a different bird. "That one is an *eaglet*," I said. "An eaglet is a baby eagle."

After that, I held my lunch box way high in the air so all of Room One could see it.

"See all the birdlets, children? There are owlets and eaglets and ducklets and chicklets," I explained.

I put my lunch box on my desk. And I took out the thermos.

"And see this thermos, people? This thermos has pictures of bird nests on it. Isn't that cute?"

May made a face.

"Ick," she said. "Who wants to drink out of a stinky, pooey bird's nest?"

I made a face at her. "*I* do, that's who, May!" I said. "I *love* drinking out of stinky, pooey birds' nests."

May reached into her desk and pulled out a lunch ticket.

"Well, I *buy* my lunch, Junie Jones," she said. "*Bought* lunches are much better than *brought* lunches. *Bought* lunches don't sit around all morning and get soggy."

I crossed my arms at that girl.

"That's the dumbest thing I ever heard of, May," I said right back. "*Brought* lunches are way better than *bought* lunches. 'Cause *brought* lunches are made special by our very own mothers!"

Mr. Scary did a frown. "Okay, okay,

girls . . . that's enough," he said.

But May kept on arguing with me.

"For your information, Junie Jones, mothers are *not* professional lunch makers," she said. "Mothers are just plain old normal people."

I stamped my foot at her. 'Cause that was my final straw!

"Do not call my mother *normal*, May!" I hollered. "No one in my whole entire family is normal! So there!"

May started to laugh.

Then some of the other children laughed, too.

I do not know why.

Finally, Mr. Scary snapped his fingers at them.

I put my lunch box back on the floor.

It was not my best morning.

2

■ ■ ■ ■ ■ ■ ■ ■ ■

Hoagies

The lunch bell rang at twelve o'clock.

Twelve o'clock is around noonish, I believe.

I picked up my lunch box and ran to the door. Then I lined up with my friends. And I waited to go.

"It's almost time," I told them very thrilled. "It's almost time for me to eat out of my brand-new lunch box!"

I held it up for them to see again.

"Which baby bird do you guys like the best?" I asked. "Pick one, okay?"

My friend named José looked at the birds and shrugged his shoulders.

"I don't know. I guess maybe I like the duck best," he said. "Ducks can be funny sometimes. One time—when we were having a picnic at the lake—a duck chased my sister and stole her Ho-Ho."

My friends Lennie and Herb laughed real hard. They looked at my lunch box, too.

"I think I like the owlet the best," said Herb.

"Me too," said Lennie. "I saw a TV show on owls once. And an owl swallowed a giant rat in just one bite. He didn't even chew or anything."

After that, I stared at Lennie a real long time.

'Cause that disgusting story just ruined my owlet, that's why.

Finally, all of Room One walked to the cafeteria together.

The cafeteria is a big room where we eat lunch. It has smells and noise and tables in it.

Room One sits near the window.

I zoomed there speedy quick.

"Come, Herb!" I called. "Come, Lennie and José! It's time for you to watch me eat out of my new lunch box!"

I turned around to wait for them.

Only too bad for me. Because none of those guys were even coming.

Instead, they were standing in the stupid dumb *lunch line*.

My mouth fell open at that sight.

"Herb! Hey, Herb!" I called. "What do you think you're doing? Why aren't you coming to eat with me?"

Herb shouted back. "I'm buying my lunch today, Junie B.!"

José shouted, too. "Me too. Everyone is buying today, Junie B.!"

"*Hoagies!* We're having *hoagies*!" hollered Lennie. "Save us a seat!"

My shoulders slumped real disappointed. 'Cause I wasn't actually expecting this development.

I sat down at my table and looked all around.

There was only one other person sitting there.

His name is Sheldon.

I do not know him that good.

Sheldon waved his fingers at me. "We're the only ones here," he said. "We're the only ones who didn't buy hoagies today."

I did a sigh. "Yes, Sheldon. I know that," I said.

Sheldon slid across from me.

"Hoagies are very popular. But I'm not allowed to eat them," he said. "I'm allergic to fake meat and cheese."

I looked at Sheldon closer.

His nose was running very much.

"Please wipe your nose," I said.

Sheldon didn't pay attention to me.

"I'm only allowed to eat food that comes from nature," he said.

His nose ran even more. "Also, I'm allergic to dairy," he told me.

I handed him my napkin. "Blow. And I mean it," I said.

Sheldon did not blow.

I slid to the end of the table.

Pretty soon, my friends started coming

out of the kitchen. The other children started coming, too.

They sat down and took big bites of their hoagies.

"Mmm," said Herb. "This hoagie is *delicious*!"

"*Sí,*" said José. "*Muy delicioso!*"

Lennie nodded. Then he opened up his hoagie roll and looked inside.

"I think even *you* would like this hoagie, Junie B.," he said. "Look. It has ham and salami and cheese and lettuce and tomato."

Just then, May butted her big head in.

"It's *good* for you, too, Junie Jones," she said. "All school lunches have to be delicious and nutritious. It's a law."

"So?" I said.

"So lunches brought from home can be any old thing," she said back.

I did a huffy breath at her.

Then I turned my back. And I hid my sandwich very secret. And I peeked inside the bread.

I stared and stared for a real long time. 'Cause I didn't actually recognize the meat, that's why.

Finally, I ate it anyway.

It was tasty . . . whatever it was.

3

Cookies

I was the first one done with my lunch.

That's because eating hoagies takes for-ever, of course.

I put my lunch box away and looked at Herb's plate.

He had three more foods to go.

First, he had carrot sticks. Also, he had applesauce and a cookie.

I leaned in closer.

"Mmm. I think that's a sugar cookie, Herbert," I said. "Sugar cookies are my favorites."

Herb nodded. "Me too," he said. "I like sugar cookies, too."

I touched his cookie with my finger.

"Yes-sir-ee-bob. That's a sugar cookie all right, Herb," I said. "I didn't get a cookie at all today. My mother packed me a fruit bar instead."

"Oh," said Herb. "Well, fruit bars are good, too."

I tapped my fingers on the table. 'Cause Herb didn't even get my hint.

"Yes, Herbert. I *know* fruit bars are good," I said. "But I really wanted a cookie today. And so I wish that you would just share that thing with me, and that's all."

Herb looked at me and shrugged. "Why didn't you just say so?" he said.

Then he broke his cookie in two. And he handed me half.

I gushed real happy. "Oh! Thank you, Herb! Thank you! Thank you!" I said.

After that, I stuffed the cookie right into my mouth. And I drank a sip of Herb's milk.

"Yum! That tasted just like the cookies that Mrs. Gutzman used to bring to afternoon kindergarten," I said.

I smiled at the thought of that woman.

"Gladys Gutzman was our snack lady last year," I explained to Herb. "She used to bring us cookies and milk every week."

I made my voice kind of secret.

"Only guess what, Herbert. Sometimes Mrs. Gutzman gave me *two* cookies instead of one," I said. "'Cause I was her favorite person in Room Nine, I think."

José heard what I said. "Hey! That must mean that I was her favorite in Room *Eight*!" he said. "Because sometimes Mrs. Gutzman gave *me* an extra one, too."

After that, me and José did a high five.

'Cause *both* of us were favorites, apparently!

"That woman was a gem, I tell you," I said.

"What do you mean she *was* a gem, Junie B.?" said José. "She still *is* a gem. Mrs. Gutzman still works here, you know."

"What?" I said very surprised.

"Sure, she does," said Herb. "I met Mrs. Gutzman this year already. She works right there in the kitchen."

I couldn't believe my ears.

"Really?" I said. "Really? Really? Really? Because if Mrs. Gutzman still works at our school, how come she hasn't brought us milk and cookies this year?"

Herb shrugged. "I don't know," he said. "But she still works here, all right. In fact, we saw her just now when we were getting our hoagies."

I put my hand over my mouth. 'Cause

that news was too good to be true!

José laughed. "If you don't believe us, go see for yourself," he said.

"I *will,* José! I *will* go see for myself!" I said real joyful.

Then I jumped right out of my seat.

And I zoomed into the kitchen.

And I hollered and hollered for Mrs. Gutzman!

4

Gladys

"Mrs. Gutzman! Mrs. Gladys Gutzman! Where are you?" I hollered. "It's me! It's me! It's Junie B. Jones!"

I looked all around me. There was a long counter with children pushing trays.

"Did anyone see Mrs. Gutzman?" I asked the children. "Does anyone know her? My friends said she is right here in this kitchen. But I don't even see her."

I hollered her name even louder.

"MRS. GUTZMAN! MRS. GLADYS GUTZMAN!"

Then, all of a sudden, a lady came hurrying around the corner.

And good news!!!

It was *her*!

It was Mrs. Gladys Gutzman!

I ran and hugged her very tight.

"Mrs. Gutzman! Mrs. Gutzman! I am so glad to see you!" I said.

Mrs. Gutzman hugged me back.

"Junie B. Jones! I'm glad to see you, too!" she said.

I smiled up at her.

She was wearing her same big white apron from last year.

"Whoa! Just look at you, Mrs. Gutzman!" I said. "You didn't change a bit!"

I patted her apron.

"You didn't even change your clothes, apparently," I said.

Mrs. Gutzman laughed.

She was wearing plastic mitts on her hands. Plus also, she was wearing a hair net.

"Hey, I remember those things from last year!" I said. "You told me that you wear plastic mitts and a hair net whenever you touch food, remember? You said that was called good hygiene. 'Cause mitts and a hair net protect our food from dirty germs and hairs."

Mrs. Gutzman made a face.

"Are you sure that's the way I put it?" she asked.

I skipped all around her in a circle.

"Hey, Mrs. Gutzman! Now that you found me, you can start bringing cookies to my room again!"

I held up one finger. "I am in Room One

this year," I said. "Room One comes earlier in the alphabet than Room Nine. And so now that you know where I am, when can you bring the cookies, Gladys?"

Mrs. Gutzman did a chuckle.

Then she leaned down next to me.

And she patted my arm.

And she said don't call her Gladys.

After that, Mrs. Gutzman explained all about snacks. She said that first graders don't get snacks like kindergarten kids do. On account of first graders get cookies with their school lunches.

I did a frown at that news.

"Yeah, only what about the children who *bring* their lunches, Mrs. Gutzman? Where's our cookies? Huh? 'Cause today everybody got a cookie except for me and Sheldon."

Mrs. Gutzman didn't answer my question. Instead, she raised her head and looked behind me.

That's when I heard my teacher's voice.

"Junie B. Jones," he said kind of loudish. "Exactly what do you think you're doing?"

I spun around.

Mr. Scary's eyes looked annoyed at me.

"Why did you get up from the table, Junie B.?" he asked. "Hmm? What's the story here?"

Everyone was staring.

I did a big gulp. Then I squeezed my eyes closed real tight. And I tried to think of the story here.

"Well, um . . . let's see," I said. "First, I was eating my *brought* lunch . . . and everyone else was eating their *bought* lunch. And so that's how come I was the first one finished. And then I was just sitting there. And I spotted Herb's sugar cookie. And I really, really wanted that thing. And good news . . . Herb *shared*! And so then that delicious cookie reminded me about Mrs. Gutzman. And what do you know? Herb and José said she was right here in this exact kitchen. So I jumped up from the table. And I ran in to say hello," I said.

After that, I looked up at Mrs. Gutzman kind of nervous. And I waved my fingers.

"Hello," I said real soft.

"Hello," she said back.

Mr. Scary shook his head. "No. I'm sorry, Junie B. I know Mrs. Gutzman has enjoyed seeing you. But you can't just get up from the table and run wherever you please during lunch," he said.

Mrs. Gutzman nodded. "Mr. Scary is right, Junie B.," she said. "I am very happy to see you. But you do have to learn to follow school rules."

I did a sigh.

"Yeah, only I really, really wanted to find you, Mrs. Gutzman," I said. "'Cause I missed you very much."

Mrs. Gutzman tapped on her chin.

"Hmm," she said. "Maybe I have an idea. Maybe—if you promise to follow the rules—you can come back tomorrow and help me in the kitchen. Would you like that, do you think?"

My eyes got big and wide at her. "Are you kidding, Mrs. Gutzman?" I said. "Is this some kind of a joke?"

She smiled again.

"Nope," she said. "It's no joke. We let children help us in the kitchen quite often. If it's okay with your teacher, I'll give you a permission slip to take home to your parents."

I pulled on Mr. Scary's arm. "Say it's okay! Okay? Please! Please! Please!" I begged.

Mr. Scary didn't answer right away.

Instead, he ran his fingers through his hair. And he thought and thought.

Then finally, he *said* it.

Mr. Scary said *it's okay*!

I clapped and danced and twirled.

"I can *do* it, Mrs. Gutzman!" I said. "I can come and help you in the kitchen!"

"Excellent!" said Mrs. Gutzman.

Then she reached behind the counter. And she handed me a permission slip.

And that is not all!

Because she reached back there one more time. And she pulled out a pair of brand-new plastic mitts!

"Here," she said. "These are for you. You can wear them around your house tonight and get used to them."

I did a gasp at those wonderful things.

"Thank you, Mrs. Gutzman! Thank

you!" I said. "I've always wanted some of these thingamajigs!"

After that, I put them on my hands very thrilled. And I waved goodbye to Mrs. Gutzman.

"See you!" I said. "See you tomorrow!"

Then I walked back to my lunch table with Mr. Scary.

And I followed the rules for the rest of the day.

5

■ ■ ■ ■ ■ ■ ■ ■ ■ ■

Practicing

After school, I ran home from my bus stop.

It was Mother's day off from work.

She was in the backyard playing with my baby brother named Ollie.

Ollie is ten months old. He cannot skip or play tag or color.

So far, I am not that satisfied with him.

I ran out the back door.

"Mother! Mother! I'm going to be a helper! I'm going to be a helper!" I shouted real cheery.

I quick handed her my permission slip.

"Read this paper! Hurry! It's from Mrs. Gutzman!" I said. "You remember Mrs. Gutzman, right? Mrs. Gutzman used to be my cookie lady last year. But this year she's branched out, apparently. 'Cause now she's the boss of the whole kitchen operation, I think."

Mother read the permission slip.

I bounced up and down very excited.

"See, Mother? See? Mrs. Gutzman wants me to be her helper in the cafeteria tomorrow. And so all you have to do is sign that paper. And I will be all set."

I started back to the house. "I'll go get you a pen!"

Mother hollered, "Hold on" to me.

"This really does sound like fun, Junie B.," she said. "But let's talk it over at dinner, okay? At dinner you can tell Daddy and me all about it."

I did a big breath at her.

"But I don't want to talk it over at dinner, Mother," I said. "I want you to sign that paper right exactly *now*. Please, please? Just sign it, okay?"

Mother smiled. "*Patience,* Junie B.," she said. "Dinner is just a few hours away.

I'd like Daddy to be in on this, too."

I rolled my eyes way up to the sky. 'Cause Daddy always has to be in on *everything*.

Finally, I went back in the house. And I walked around the kitchen very bored.

"There's not even anything to do in this stupid dumb house," I grouched.

Then, all of a sudden, I spotted my backpack sitting on the floor.

That's when I remembered my plastic mitts!

I'd put them in my backpack to carry them home from school!

I hurried to get them out of there.

Then I quick put them on. And I ran to the refrigerator.

"Now I can practice touching food!" I said real thrilled.

I opened up the door and started touching stuff.

First, I touched some fruit, and an avocado, and a squishy tomato. Then I put my hand in the butter. And also some creamy cottage cheese.

"Whoa. These mitts make touching food enjoyable," I said.

After I was done, I put the mitts in my pocket. And I went to watch TV. Only I couldn't even pay attention that good. 'Cause I kept on thinking about being a helper, of course.

My excitement got bigger and bigger.

Then hurray, hurray! Daddy finally came home from work! And it was time for dinner!

As soon as I sat down, I told Daddy all about Mrs. Gutzman.

Then surprise! I put on my mitts. And I waved my hands all around in the air.

"Look, Mother! Look, Daddy! See what Mrs. Gutzman gave me? These are real professional mitts from the actual cafeteria!"

I sat up straight and tall. "Mitts do not spread dirty germs," I explained. "And guess what else? I already know how to use these babies."

After that, I jumped down from my chair. And I ran around the table. And I touched everyone's dinner.

I touched Mother's meatloaf. And Daddy's mashed potatoes. And Ollie's creamed corn.

Also, I put creamed corn on Ollie's head.

That was a funny joke, I think. Only no one even laughed.

Mother took my mitts away.

She said that is not what mitts are for, young lady.

At first, I thought I was in very big trouble. But more good news!

When Mother and Daddy tucked me in bed that night, they gave me back my permission slip. And hurray! It was signed!

"We're going to let you help in the kitchen," said Mother. "But no more funny business with the mitts. Got it?"

"Got it," I said.

"A helper doesn't make things more difficult, Junie B.," said Daddy. "A helper makes things easier. Okay?"

"Okay," I said.

Mother made her eyes real serious. "And a helper is *not* the boss, Junie B.," she said. "Maybe you should try repeating that one. A helper is *not* the boss."

I repeated it.

"A helper is not the boss," I said. "A helper is not the boss."

After that, Mother and Daddy looked calmer. They kissed me good night and turned off my light.

I repeated it one more time.

"A helper is not the boss," I said.

Then I closed my eyes.

And I went to sleep.

And I dreamed I was the boss.

6

Boss of Lunch

It was the funnest dream I ever had.

I looked exactly like Mrs. Gutzman. Except I had my own face.

Also, I had my own apron. And my own plastic mitts. And my very own hair net.

I was a vision, I tell you!

I worked my hardest in the kitchen.

I washed all the carrots. And I made all the hoagies. Plus also, I ate all the sugar cookies.

After a while, Room One came into the kitchen with their trays.

The children saw how hard I was working.

They called me "Boss of Lunch." And they skipped around me in a happy circle.

After that, they carried me all around on their shoulders.

May did not participate.

I waved at her when I went by.

Then a duck flew in and chased her out of the room.

That morning, I woke up laughing in my pillow.

And guess what else? At school, my day kept on getting better and better. Because I gave Mr. Scary my permission slip. And he let me go to the cafeteria at ten o'clock A.M.! And so I hardly even did much work!

Mrs. Gutzman was delighted to see me again.

She said I could start helping her very soon. But first she wanted to show me around the kitchen.

It was the hugest kitchen I ever even saw.

It was a kitchen a *giant* would have.

"Look at how big everything is, Mrs. Gutzman," I said. "Look at that big dishwasher over there. And look at those big refrigerators! And whoa! Look at those big sinks! And that big giant freezer!"

I kept looking. "And look at that big can opener. And look at this big floor we're standing on. And look at these big walls. And that big light switch. And those big—"

Mrs. Gutzman interrupted me.

"Okay, let's move on, shall we?" she said. "I'd like you to meet some of the other folks who work here, Junie B."

After that, she took me over and introduced me to six grownups.

I waved at those people kind of shy.

They waved back. Plus also, they said "welcome."

But here is the bestest part of all! After I met all the people, Mrs. Gutzman opened a big drawer. And she handed me a giant white apron!

My mouth fell open at that hugie thing!

"You mean I get to wear this, Mrs. Gutzman?" I said. "I get to wear an apron just like yours? Wowie wow wow! This is my dream come true!"

Mrs. Gutzman winked at me.

"Well, we sure don't want you to mess

up that pretty flowered dress of yours, do we?" she said.

After that, she pulled the apron over my head. And she tied the straps around me.

I looked down to the ground. The apron came down to my shoes, almost.

I twirled and twirled all around.

"Oooh! I *love* this apron, Mrs. Gutzman!" I said. "This apron makes me feel like a princess!"

Mrs. Gutzman said I had a good imagination.

After that, I put on my mitts that she had given me. And I twirled some more.

"Now I have the whole complete outfit, practically!" I said real happy.

And then, what do you know? All of a sudden, Mrs. Gutzman reached into her apron. And she pulled out a hair net!

A hair net just for me!

She put it on my head.

"Oh boy! Oh boy! Thank you, Mrs. Gutzman! Thank you!" I squealed.

Then I zoomed to the oven and stared at myself in the glass.

"Look at me! Just look at me! I look like a real professional lunch maker!" I said.

After that, I stared and stared at myself some more.

And I couldn't even stop.

7

Jobs

Pretty soon, Mrs. Gutzman told me all about my jobs.

"You're going to have three fun jobs today, Junie B.," she said. "I think you're going to like all of them."

She took me to the long counter where the children push their lunch trays. And she showed me where the napkins go.

"Your first job will be to keep napkins stacked up right here on the countertop. If the napkin piles start to run out, just reach under the counter and get more. Okay? Do

you think you can do that for me, Junie
B.?"

I nodded real fast. "Yes!" I said. "I
know I can do that, Mrs. Gutzman! 'Cause
I'm already familiar with napkins!"

I smiled real proud. "I use napkins at my
very own house," I said. "I use them to
wipe my mouth after dinner. Plus sometimes, I use my sleeve."

Mrs. Gutzman looked funny at me.

After that, she handed me a sponge and took me to the counter by the sinks.

"Okay. Your second job will be to keep this big counter wiped off," she said. "You don't have to clean any big messes, Junie B. Just wipe up any little spills or crumbs you see."

I grinned real big.

"Sponges are another job I am good at, Mrs. Gutzman," I said. "'Cause one time in kindergarten, I practiced throwing sponges in my toilet. And I didn't even miss the pot, hardly."

Mrs. Gutzman's face went kind of pale.

"Oh," she said. "Oh my."

After that, her voice sounded a little bit worried.

"Well, uh . . . there's just one more job I need to tell you about," she said. "Do you see that door over there? That's where the children come in the kitchen to get their lunches."

"Yes," I said. "I see it."

"Well—when you're not busy with your other jobs—I'd like you to be our lunch greeter," she said. "Do you know what a greeter is, Junie B.? A greeter smiles at people and says hello. Do you think you could do that?"

This time, I didn't answer her right away. 'Cause that job made my stomach feel jumpy inside.

"Yeah, only there's children who I don't even know at this school, Mrs. Gutzman," I said kind of shaky. "And some of them are big kids. And *big* kids are not my favorite size."

Mrs. Gutzman did a chuckle.

"Don't worry, Junie B. I think you'll find there are lots of very *nice* big kids at this school," she said. "Could you just give it a try, please?"

I shrugged my shoulders kind of weakish.

"I don't know . . . maybe I could," I said.

Mrs. Gutzman gave me a pat. "That's the spirit," she said. "Now there's just one other thing we need to talk about before you get started."

Then guess what? She reached under the counter. And she gave me *another* pair of mitts.

I quick held up my hands for her to see.

"But I'm already *wearing* mitts, Mrs. Gutzman. See them? You already gave them to me yesterday."

"I know. But these are brand-new ones, Junie B.," she said. "Around here, we change our plastic mitts quite often. That's how we keep from spreading germs. We're constantly washing our hands and changing our mitts."

I scratched my head.

"No kidding," I said. "Really? You

mean I'm supposed to wash my hands, *plus* wear mitts? My, my. That's a lot of hygiene, isn't it?"

Mrs. Gutzman did a teensy frown.

Then she took me to the sink. And she washed my hands real good.

After they were dry, she put the new mitts on me.

"Whoa. These are the cleanest hands I ever saw," I said.

After that, I skipped back to the counter. And I began stacking napkins.

Pretty soon, the kitchen started getting smells in it.

I sniffed the air.

The smells were not delicious.

"P.U.," I said kind of quiet.

Mrs. Gutzman looked over at me.

I held my nose.

"I smell stinkle," I said.

Mrs. Gutzman did not look happy. "Holding your nose isn't sanitary, Junie B. Now you'll have to change your mitts again."

I kept on holding my nose.

"Yes, but if I let go of my nose, the stinkle will get in my nostrils," I explained. "And that smell is not delightful."

Mrs. Gutzman looked annoyed at me.

"What you're smelling is our *lunch* today, Junie B.," she said. "We're baking tuna noodle casserole. We're going to be serving it with carrots and peas."

I made a sick face.

"Bluck," I said. "I hate peas. It's a good thing I brought my lunch today. Right, Mrs. Gutzman? At least now I will get a decent meal."

Mrs. Gutzman still looked grumpity.

She came over and changed my mitts.

After that, I stacked more napkins.

And I tried to just breathe through my mouth.

8

Lunchtime

Being a helper is not a breeze.

After the lunch bell rang, big kids started coming into the kitchen.

Two of them pointed at my hair net.

They called me the name of Freak-a-zoid.

I felt very crumbling inside. "Now I'm not even going to greet you," I said real quiet.

After that, I tattletaled to Mrs. Gutzman. And she grouched at those boys. Plus also, she said I didn't have to greet people.

Instead, she said I could sponge the counter.

I hurried over there my fastest.

Then I sponged and sponged until the big kids were gone.

Pretty soon, I looked at the door again.

And guess what?

I saw my friends from Room One!

I saw Herb and Lennie and José and Shirley and Roger! They were at the counter with their trays!

I ran over to them speedy quick.

"Hello, everyone! Hello! Hello! Look at me! See me working in here? I am being a helper! See?" I said.

All of them smiled and waved. "Hi, Junie B.! Hi!" they said.

I skipped around in a circle.

"See my outfit? I am a real professional

lunch maker! See? I look just like Mrs. Gutzman!"

I showed them my sponge. "And look at this! I even have *'quipment*!"

After that, I ran back to the sinks. And I showed them how I wiped the counter.

"Can everyone see me over here?" I asked. "I am the boss of this whole entire sponged area."

After that, I zoomed to the napkins.

"Plus also, I am the boss of the napkins," I said. "See how I stacked them? If I keep up the good work, someday I will be the boss of this whole operation, probably!"

Just then, May came in the door.

She did a mean laugh.

"You're not a *real* lunch maker, Junie

Jones," she said. "They're just letting you *pretend*. Don't you know that?"

All of a sudden, I felt steamy mad inside.

'Cause I am sick and tired of that dumb girl!

I stamped my foot real hard.

"Yes, I am, *too,* a real lunch maker!" I said. "Can't you even see my outfit, May? If I am not a real lunch maker, then how come I am wearing mitts and a hair net? Huh?"

May did not answer.

"I'LL TELL YOU WHY, SISTER!" I said. "'CAUSE I'M KEEPING HAIR AND GERMS OUT OF THE TUNA NOODLE STINKLE! THAT'S WHY!"

Behind me, I heard Mrs. Gutzman groan.

I turned around to see her.

Her face looked very sickish.

I turned back to Room One.

Their faces looked sickish, too.

One by one, all of them put their lunch trays back.

"I don't really feel that hungry anymore," said Herb kind of quiet.

"Me neither," said José. "I had a really big breakfast."

Then, very slow, all of the children started backing out of the kitchen.

I watched them from the door.

They backed all the way to our lunch table.

Mr. Scary was waiting for them there.

He talked to them a minute. Then he came into the kitchen and talked to Mrs. Gutzman.

They whispered to each other for a real long time.

Also, they kept looking at me. And they wouldn't even stop.

My head got drops of sweaty on it.

I wiped it off with my sponge.

After that, Mrs. Gutzman closed her eyes again.

Then she walked to me very nice.

And she took away my sponge.

And she said my job was done.

9

Baloney

Monday

Dear first-grade journal,

Room One is still mad at me about Friday.

After we went back to the room, Mrs. Gutzman brought baloney ~~baloony~~ sandwiches for the children who didn't eat.

They were not a hit.

I sat at my desk. And I ate

out of my new lunch box. I had
a tasty peanut butter and jelly
sandwich. 'Cause <u>brought</u> lunch
is better than <u>bought</u> lunch.
And that is not even my fault.
   Some of the children watched
me eat. They made growly
faces at me.
   Today Herbert is my only
friend.
   Also, Lennie and José are
being ~~resonable~~ reasonable.
   I wish Friday never
happened.
            From,
         Junie B., First Grader

I peeked my eyes at the clock.

It was almost two-fifteen.

Just one more hour before I could go home.

I tried to make the clock go faster with my eyes. It did not actually work that good.

Just then, there was a knock on our door.

Mr. Scary answered it.

"Why, hello!" he said.

"Why, hello yourself," said a friendly voice.

And guess what?

It was Mrs. Gutzman!

She walked in the room with two boxes in her arms.

My heart pounded and pounded to see that woman. 'Cause what if she came to scold me?

I slumped way down in my seat so she couldn't see me.

Mrs. Gutzman set the boxes on Mr. Scary's desk.

Then she looked all around the room.

I slumped in my seat even farther.

Only too bad for me. Because Blabber-mouth May pointed at me.

"MRS. GUTZMAN! MRS. GUTZ-MAN!" she hollered. "JUNIE JONES IS TRYING TO HIDE FROM YOU! SHE IS SLIDING DOWN IN HER CHAIR SO YOU CAN'T SEE HER! BUT I AM KEEP-ING TRACK OF HER MOVEMENTS!"

After that, I slid all the way to the floor under my desk.

I curled into a ball and hid my head.

Pretty soon, I heard feet walking to my desk.

I am getting used to that sound.

The feet stopped next to my chair.

I opened one eye and peeked out.

I saw the bottom of Mrs. Gutzman's white apron.

"Junie B.?" said her voice. "Why are you sitting on the floor?"

I didn't move any muscles.

'Cause maybe she would still go away, possibly.

"Junie B.?" said Mrs. Gutzman again. "I brought something for your class. Don't you want to see what it is?"

I shook my head real fast. "No, thank you," I said. "I don't want to see it. And so you can be on your way now, please."

I opened my other eye and looked at her feet. They kept on standing there.

Then, all of a sudden, I heard a loud groan. And what do you know? That woman squatted right down next to me!

I was shocked to see her.

"Mrs. Gutzman!" I said. "What are you doing down here?"

Mrs. Gutzman did not look comfortable.

"Please, Junie B. I need your help," she said. "I brought cookies for your class

72

today. But there's no one up there to help
me pass them out."

I rolled my eyes way back in my head.
'Cause that was not even the truth, of
course.

"Yes, there is, Mrs. Gutzman," I said.
"There's *lots* of people up there to help
you."

Mrs. Gutzman shook her head. "No, no.
You don't understand," she said.

After that, she reached into her pocket. And she pulled out a pair of plastic mitts.

"I need a *real* helper, Junie B.," she said. "I need someone with *experience*."

Mrs. Gutzman smiled kind of painful.

"Please," she said. "If we don't stand soon, I'm going to fall right on my keister, and you'll *never* get me up."

I did a teensy smile. 'Cause that was a little joke, I believe.

Finally, I crawled out from my desk. And I helped Mrs. Gutzman stand up.

"I *guess* I can help you pass out cookies," I said kind of quiet. "But some of these children are still very mad at me, you know."

Mrs. Gutzman held my hand. "Yes, well, I think maybe I can fix that," she said.

After that, me and her walked to the

front of the room together. And Mrs. Gutzman showed everyone the cookies.

"Sugar cookies!" shouted the children. "Thank you, Mrs. Gutzman! Thank you!"

Mrs. Gutzman put her hand on my shoulder.

"Don't thank *me*, class," she said. "Junie B. Jones is the one who reminded me to pay you a visit this year. *She's* the one you need to thank."

For a second no one said anything. Then, all of a sudden, Herb hollered out *thank you, Junie B. Jones!* And then all of the other children hollered *thank you*, too!

I grinned real big. 'Cause those words felt happy in my ears.

After that, I hurried back to the sink and washed my hands. Then I quick put on my mitts and ran back.

Mrs. Gutzman gave me a thumbs-up.

"Ready to go, helper?" she said.

"Ready to go!" I said back.

And so then both of us passed out all of the cookies together.

And I did a perfect job!

And so here is what I am thinking.

I am thinking that maybe someday I won't be the Boss of Lunch after all.

Maybe someday I will just be the Boss of *Cookies* instead!

Because Boss of Cookies is the most delicious job I ever heard of!

Plus also, I will get to make all the

cookie rules! And I have already thought of Rule Number One!

I wrote it in my journal so I won't forget it.

RULE NUMBER ONE

1. The Boss of Cookies gets to have ~~8~~ ~~✳~~ ⑤ sugar cookies all to herself!

P.S. Only never eat them in front of the children. 'Cause that would be rude, probably.

(P.S. again) Plus sometimes she can even eat ☆6☆! HA!

The end.

BARBARA PARK is one of today's funniest, most popular authors. Her middle-grade novels, which include *Skinnybones*, *The Kid in the Red Jacket*, *My Mother Got Married (And Other Disasters)*, and *Mick Harte Was Here*, have won over forty children's book awards. Barbara holds a B.S. in education from the University of Alabama. She has two grown sons and lives with her husband, Richard, in Arizona.

DENISE BRUNKUS'S entertaining illustrations have appeared in over fifty books. She lives in New Jersey with her husband and daughter.